This book is a gift from

THE SOHO CENTER

www.child2000.org

and

UNIVERSITY *of* VIRGINIA
Children's Hospital

www.UVAChildrensHospital.com

For great children's literacy tips,
please visit
www.child2000.org/literacy

P9-DGE-630

This book is dedicated
to my favorite football players of all time:
JOE NAMATH, LARRY CSONKA, and REGGIE WHITE

Henry Holt and Company, LLC
PUBLISHERS SINCE 1866
175 Fifth Avenue
New York, New York 10010
mackids.com

Henry Holt® is a registered trademark of Henry Holt and Company, LLC.
Copyright © 2013 by Peter McCarty
All rights reserved.

Library of Congress Cataloging-in-Publication Data
McCarty, Peter, author, illustrator.
Fall ball / Peter McCarty. — First edition.
   pages   cm
Summary: "Bobby and his friends wait all day for school to end and for their chance to play outdoors
in the fall weather. Flying leaves, swirling colors, and crisp air make the perfect setting for a game
of football with Sparky the dog. The kids are surprised by how quickly it gets dark, and even more
surprised when it begins to snow. But there's no need to worry—the chilly nights ahead will mean
watching football on the couch with family, tucked under a cozy blanket" —Provided by publisher.
ISBN 978-0-8050-9253-0 (hardcover)
[1. Autumn—Fiction. 2. Football—Fiction.] I. Title.
PZ7.M47841327Fal 2013   [E]—dc23   2013009202

Henry Holt books may be purchased for business or promotional use. For information
on bulk purchases, please contact Macmillan Corporate and Premium Sales Department
at (800) 221-7945 x5442 or by e-mail at specialmarkets@macmillan.com.

First Edition—2013 / Designed by Patrick Collins
The artist used pen, ink, and watercolors on watercolor paper to create the illustrations for this book.
Printed in China by South China Printing Co. Ltd., Dongguan City, Guangdong Province
10 9 8 7 6 5 4 3 2

FALL BALL

PETER McCARTY

Henry Holt and Company
New York

In the fall, leaves whirl past the windows of the big yellow bus.

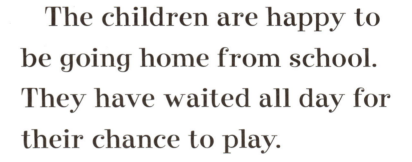

The children are happy to be going home from school. They have waited all day for their chance to play.

Along country lanes, past one fat cow,
the school bus rattles along.

The bus sails over a hill.

Whoa! The children feel
like they are floating
in the air.

The school bus stops.

"Everybody out," says the driver.

"Careful now."

"Hooray!" shout the children.
They are home at last.

"Okay, football in the park
in ten minutes!" Bobby says.

"Hi, Mom. I'm home!" Bobby shouts. "I'm going to the park now. But I'll be back when it's dark."

"Come on, Jimmy. Time for football!" says Bobby.
"Nah, look at all these leaves," Jimmy says.

"Hey, Sparky. Watch it!"

"Everyone ready?" says Bobby.

"Let's play ball!"

Bobby goes back to pass.

The ball flies through the air...

...and **Sparky** runs away with the ball!

"Hey, Sparky. Come back!"

CRASH!

Right into the pile
of leaves!

"Jimmy! Brian! Ethan!
JASON! Katie!
Vincent!
Suki! Bobby!

MARTIN!

Time to come home!"

"Time to go home?"
"Already?"

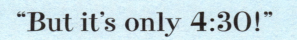

"But it's only 4:30!"